Caring for Your Magical Pets

Taking Care of Your

Eric Braun

BLACK RABBIT BOOKS

Hi Jinx is published by Black Rabbit Books
P.O. Box 3263, Mankato, Minnesota, 56002.
www.blackrabbitbooks.com
Copyright © 2020 Black Rabbit Books

Marysa Storm, editor; Michael Sellner, designer;
Omay Ayres, photo researcher

Library of Congress Cataloging-in-Publication Data
Names: Braun, Eric, 1971- author, illustrator.
Title: Taking care of your dragon / by Eric Braun.
Description: Mankato, Minnesota : Black Rabbit Books, [2020]
Series: Hi Jinx. Caring for your magical pets | Includes bibliographical
references and index. | Summary: Provides easy-to-read instructions for
choosing and caring for a pet dragon, as well as the hazards of owning
a large, fire-breathing beast. Includes discussion questions. | Includes
bibliographical references and index.
Identifiers: LCCN 2018040256 (print) | LCCN 2018051475 (ebook) |
ISBN 9781680729160 (e-book) | ISBN 9781680729108 (library binding) |
ISBN 9781644660898 (paperback)
Subjects: | CYAC: Dragons–Fiction. | Pets–Fiction.
Classification: LCC PZ7.1.B751542 (ebook) | LCC PZ7.1.B751542 Tak 2020
(print) | DDC [E]–dc23
LC record available at https://lccn.loc.gov/2018040256

Printed in China. 1/19

Image Credits

iStock: bauhaus1000, 20 (dino); Shutterstock: Alena Kozlova, 12–13 (hill);
alexmstudio, Cover (bkgd), 11 (bkgd); Aluna1, 8 (bkgd); AnggaR3ind, 10
(poop), 11 (poop); Artoshka, 15 (top dragon); ChristianPhoenix, 2–3; Christos
Georghiou, 19, DM7, 16–17 (dragon); Gorban, 15 (btm dragons); GraphicsRF,
17; Julien Tromeur, 20 (dragon), 21 (dragon); Lilu330, 4 (dragons), 5 (dragon);
Malchev, 6–7; mejnak, 12 (bkgd); Memo Angeles, Cover (girl, dragons), 1
(boy, dragon), 8–9, 9 (girl, dragon), 11 (girl, dragons), 15 (girl, suds), 23 (boy,
dragon); NextMars, 4 (bkgd), 16–17 (bkgd); opicobello, 8 (tear), 9 (marker
strokes), 10 (tear); Pasko Maksim, Back Cover (tear), 7 (tear), 11 (tear), 23 (top),
24; petroleum man, Cover (spray), 11 (spray); Pitju, Back Cover (bkgd), 3 (bkgd),
16 (curl), 21 (bkgd, curl); Ron Dale, 5 (marker stroke), 6 (marker stroke), 10
(marker stroke), 20; Ron Leishman, 12 (dragon, cat), 13; Sukhonosova Anastasia,
1 (fire), 23 (fire); totallypic, 6 (arrow), 7 (arrow); Victor Brave, Cover (hose),
11 (hose); your, 6–7 (clouds), zooco, 6 (dragon) Every effort has been made to
contact copyright holders for material reproduced in this book. Any omissions
will be rectified in subsequent printings if notice is given to the publisher.

Contents

4

Chapter 1

Is a Dragon Right for You?

A baby dragon runs and plays. It jumps into the air, testing out its wings. Flap, flap, flap. The dragon goes a few feet before rolling onto the ground. It isn't ready to fly just yet!

Falling in love with dragons at pet stores is easy. They're so cute! But remember they grow up. Dragons can be sweet and **loyal** pets. But owners must know what they're getting into. Bringing home a dragon will change your life.

Chapter 2
Understanding Your Dragon

Before getting a dragon, you must decide what type best fits your lifestyle. All dragons are winged **reptiles**. But there are many different **species**. Some have powerful back legs and **muscular** shoulders. These are **classic** dragons. Other dragons are more like snakes. They are long and thin.

An example of a classic dragon is the Hydra. This dragon has many heads. Dragons with more than one head are best for experienced dragon owners.

Snakelike dragons are the quietest. Dragons with many heads can be chatty. Their heads talk to each other.

The Strong and Silent Type

In the wild, most dragons live alone. They are not **social** creatures. It takes time for any dragon to make friends. But once they do, dragons are very loyal.

Many dragons can talk. But you might never know it. Dragons are quiet and thoughtful. They often keep their ideas to themselves.

Chapter 3
Caring for your Dragon

Understanding your dragon is just the beginning. You must also know how to care for it.

First of all, you'll need lots of space. You can keep your baby dragon in your home. But soon, your dragon will get bigger. You'll need a barn or large garage.

You'll also need to hire a dump truck service to pick up poop. Have it come every week.

Finally, you must remember that dragons can breathe fire. Sometimes they sneeze fireballs. Watch out!

Keep several fire extinguishers handy at all times. Young dragons can have a hard time controlling their firepower.

11

Feeding

Like other animals, dragons need fresh water and food. Dragons like meat. And they eat lots of it. They'll need more and more as they get bigger and bigger. Feeding a dragon isn't cheap. But don't skimp! If your dragon goes to bed hungry, it'll hunt **local** pets. Your neighbors will not like that. Neither will the police.

Cleaning and Playing

Most dragons keep themselves clean. Your dragon will only need a monthly bath. Be sure to use warm water and scale-friendly soap.

Believe it or not, dragons like to play. Dragon toys aren't like other pets' toys, though. They like gold and jewels. A pile of riches to guard will keep them happy.

Most dragons live hundreds of years. This pet will be in your family for a long time.

Exercising

Dragons need exercise. To exercise, dragons must stretch their wings and fly. They should fly for at least one hour each day. Flying daily keeps them healthy.

A Lifelong Friend

Owning a dragon is a lot of work. Most people are better off getting a dog or cat. But if you want a challenge, a dragon could be for you. Just remember to treat your dragon well, and it'll be happy. It'll become a lifelong friend.

Chapter 4
Get in on the
Hi Jinx

Dragons aren't real. But they're fun to imagine. In fact, stories about dragons go back hundreds of years. The stories probably started when **ancient** people found dinosaur bones. They didn't know of any creature with bones that big. So they imagined dragons. People still tell stories about dragons today. Some movies and TV shows have evil dragons. Others show them as friendly helpers.

Take It One Step More

1. Books, movies, and TV shows about dragons are popular. Why do you think that is?

2. Would you fly on a dragon? Why or why not?

3. Dragons are evil in many stories. Why do you think that is?

GLOSSARY

ancient (AYN-shunt)—from a time
long ago

classic (KLAS-ik)—being typical or usual
of its kind

local (LOH-kuhl)—a person or thing who
lives in a particular area, city, or town

loyal (LOY-uhl)—having complete support
for someone or something

muscular (MUS-kyu-lur)—having large
and strong muscles

reptile (REP-tile)—a cold-blooded animal
that breathes air and has a backbone; most
reptiles lay eggs and have scaly skin.

social (SO-shul)—liking to be with and
talk to others

species (SPEE-seez)—a class of individuals
that have common characteristics and share
a common name

BOOKS

Alberti, Theresa Jarosz. *Dragons.* Mythical Creatures. Lake Elmo, MN: Focus Readers, 2019.

Loh-Hagan, Virginia. *Dragons: Magic, Myth, and Mystery.* Magic, Myth, and Mystery. Ann Arbor, MI: Cherry Lake Publishing, 2017.

Szymanski, Jennifer. *Real Dragons.* National Geographic Reader. Washington, DC: National Geographic Kids, 2018.

WEBSITES

Dragon Facts and Myths with Disney's Pete's Dragon
www.funkidslive.com/new/dragon-facts-myths-disneys-petes-dragon/#

Dragons
www.factmonster.com/features/creature-catalog/dragons

Ten Real-Life Animals that Are Dragons
www.bbc.com/earth/story/20150426-ten-amazing-real-life-dragons

INDEX